Franklin B. Wiley

Roadside Rhymes

Franklin B. Wiley

Roadside Rhymes

ISBN/EAN: 9783337272005

Printed in Europe, USA, Canada, Australia, Japan

Cover: Foto ©Andreas Hilbeck / pixelio.de

More available books at **www.hansebooks.com**

FRANKLIN BALDWIN WILEY

ROADSIDE RHYMES

Plorem artis in te nil agentis exitus?

HORACE.

CAMBRIDGE
CHARLES W. SEVER
University Bookstore
1885

University Press:
JOHN WILSON AND SON, CAMBRIDGE.

CONTENTS.

iv CONTENTS.

ROADSIDE RHYMES.

Short swallow-flights of song.

TENNYSON.

ROADSIDE RHYMES.

THE IDEAL WORLD.

WHEN twinkling stars in twilight skies
   Contend with day's departing beam,
The Ideal World's fair portals rise
   Mid golden glow and silvery gleam:
And they, who pass its pearly gates,
   Attain a land of perfect peace,
Where heavenly bliss forever waits,
   And earthly woes forever cease;
And storms ne'er cloud the welkin's blue,
   Nor lash to foam the sapphire seas;
But softly drops the nightly dew,
   And sweetly blows the fragrant breeze;

And beauty broods o'er hill, and cave,
    And field, and dell forevermore ;
And music steals from every wave
    That ripples up the curving shore.

No Summers shed a sultry glare
    On dusty plains and wilting bowers;
No Autumns fill the mournful air
    With falling leaves and withered flowers;
No Winters freeze the flowing streams,
    And darkly drive the drifting snow;
Eternal Spring forever beams
    From stars above on flowers below:
For subtle change, and slow decay,
    And grim destruction cannot mar
A single bud, or leaf, or spray,
    Nor quench a solitary star;
But far beyond those gates of pearl
    The vales extend, the plains expand,
And time and death can ne'er unfurl
    Their standards in that lovely land.

Each year, each month, each fleeting day,
  Each passing minute's headlong flight,
Bears something from our lives away
  To flourish in those fields of light;
Each glory of the growing past
  Seeks refuge in that world of bliss,
Whose widening bounds grow yet more vast
  With every moment fled from this:
There envy's sneer and hatred's frown
  Are banished from each blissful face,
And foiled ambition finds the crown
  It lost in its terrestrial race;
There mercy dries the mourner's tear,
  And smooths the wrinkled brow of care ·
And every form that faded here
  In deathless life is blooming there.

Ah, when the silver evening-star
  Allures our unreluctant feet
From this world's harsh, incessant jar
  To that serene and still retreat,

And all our woes and all our cares —
   Like Christian's burden — disappear
Before the soft and soothing airs
   That wander through that happy sphere,
How sweet the oft recurring thought
   That when our low descending sun
At last attains the goal it sought,
   And life's eventful day is done, —
Perchance beyond the fatal stream,
   Within the gates by angels pearled,
We may complete this earthly dream
   And find in heaven our Ideal World.

AD FINEM.

[C. E. W.]

O for the touch of a vanish'd hand,
And the sound of a voice that is still!
TENNYSON.

HER latest breath is drawn:
Her dove-like soul hath ta'en its skyward flight,
And greets the glory of an endless dawn
Beyond the gates of light.

Long years have silvered o'er
The dark brown tresses of her youth's bright Spring,
And pierced her bosom to its inmost core
With sorrow's deadly sting.

Ay, grief, and care, and toil
Have left their trace upon that furrowed brow;
Yet virtue's flowers within her soul's deep soil
    Blossomed as passed the plough.

Adversity's dark cloud
But dropped its shower of wisdom on her mind;
And when distress's thunders echoed loud
    Her heart was strong and kind.

Her smile was as a light
That sheds a cheering radiance over all,
And scatters through the shadows of the night
    Its mute, inspiring call.

When hope with flickering ray
Had nearly ceased to light life's troubled flood,
Unshaken in her faith she still could say,
    " His loving kindness, O how good! "

And when misfortunes came
Till her bowed form could scarce sustain their weight,
Through whitening lips her whispers were the same —
    " His loving kindness, O how great! "

Life's skies became serene,
And its vast ocean calm as summer sea,
And still she gladly sang, with grateful mien,
    " His loving kindness, O how free ! "

Year after year flew by,
Yet ever floated her unvaried song
In strains of sweetest rapture to the sky —
    " His loving kindness, O how strong ! "

And when the hour drew nigh
Whose gloomy close received her parting breath,
Amid the saddened hush her last faint sigh
    " His loving kindness sung in death."

Y^E SONGE OF Y^E TROUBADOUR.

O LOVERS maie rave of their Mystresses' Eyes,
& yeeld to ye Brownest or Blackest ye Prize;
But neither soe quicklye can waken a Sighe
As ye Sunshiny Glance of a Bonnie Bleue Eye.

'T wil melte in one Ogle a Bosom of Stone,
& force it Love's Magicall Passion to owne;
Then Who wolde not baske, tho' it cost him a Sighe,
In ye Hearte-thryllynge Beam of a Bonnie Bleue Eye?

'T wil laughe in Delighte, & 't wil kyndle in Love
Til it glowes lyke ye Sunne in ye Azure above;
Then Who wolde not turne from ye Brightest Bleue Sky
To gaze in ye Heaven of a Bonnie Bleue Eye?

In Sorrow 't wil weepe, & in Pitie 't wil beam
Lyke a Brighte-cheering Raie o'er a Darke-flowing Streame;
Then Who wolde not languish in Pain juste to lie
In yᵉ Softe, Tender Lighte of a Bonnie Bleue Eye?

Iff Plato sholde looke from yᵉ Regions above,
He'd forgett his Fantasticall Notions of Love,
& quicklye wolde alle his Philosophic flye
In yᵉ Soule-styrrynge Gaze of a Bonnie Bleue Eye.

Soe Lovers maie rave of their Mystresses' Eyes,
& yeeld to yᵉ Brownest or Blackest yᵉ Prize;
But neither soe quicklye can waken a Sighe
As Heaven's Beste Mirror — a Bonnie Bleue Eye.

INTERCESSION.

August 29, 1879.

OLIVER WENDELL HOLMES, BORN AUGUST 29, 1809.

TOUCH gently, Time, his heart whose flow
   Has filled the years with strains of sweetness —
Whose morning flush, whose noonday glow
   Melt into evening's bright completeness:
His fading locks — O tell us, Time,
   Thy frosty breath this change has wrought 'em,
But that beneath the crusted rime
   Repose the ripened fruits of Autumn.

And thou, kind Nature, though we know
   His life has filled thine olden measure,
Let health delay the hand of snow
   Which numbing death extends at pleasure.
To-day he reaps what he has sown
   At festal board and friendly meeting;
The harvest of his life is mown
   And garnered in a nation's greeting.

THE CORAL SPRAY.

FAR down in the depths of the dark blue sea,
　Where the waters hardly sway,
Where the goldfish glides with a sportive glee,
　There once was a coral spray:
Of a pearly pink was its surface tinct;
　Its form was of matchless grace;
And ambition gave it the high instinct
　That belongs to the human race.

"How I loathe the quiet that reigns around!
　How I long to rise and be free —
To look down where the frothy billows bound,
　That so long have looked down on me!"

2

So it summoned the coral insect hordes,
  And bade them begin to build;
It pierced the brine with its roseate swords
  Till the workers grew numb and chilled.

In sunlight and shadow the sea moaned on;
  Moon after moon waxed and waned;
Many a star from the sky was gone,
  In their places new orbs reigned;
And ships sailed over the desolate main,
  Or sank amid sailors' cries;
But the coral spray, with a cold disdain,
  Ever continued to rise;

Till at last, as it upward wreathed its arms
  Through the green and glassy brine,
Lo! playing over its glistening charms
  Did a sunbeam softly shine;
But scarce had it felt the genial glow,
  That shot to its inmost core,
When the black clouds over the sky did blow,
  And the sunbeam shone no more.

The angry billows, with furious roar,
  Swept over the coral spray,
Till a rudderless ship, as she onward tore,
  Broke the trembling thing away:
Down, down it hurried! But, as it sank,
  Rang agonized human tones;
The crack of the spar, the crash of the plank,
  Were followed by gurgling groans.

Far down in the depths of the dark blue sea,
  Where the waters hardly sway,
Where the goldfish glides with a sportive glee,
  There glistens a coral spray:
Beside it a sailor lies stiff and stark,
  Asleep on the ocean floor;
He will rise one day from his slumbers dark,
  But the spray will rise no more.

EROS.

A NEWE SONGE IN OLDE CLOATHES.

In my Hearte there hath nestled a Beinge of Lighte
  Synce ye Momente I lookt upon Thee;
In Thy Smyle is its Daie, in Thy Frowne is its Nighte:
  Canst Thou guesse Who y^s Beinge maie be?

Its Heaven is ye Bleue of Thy beautyfulle Eyes,
  & it seekes for its twyn Brother there;
But soe calme is their Gaze, soe complete their Dysguise,
  Y^t it shrynkes from their Glance in Despayre.

Yett it lives but for Thee, & withe Thee it wolde die,
  For my Hearte wolde soone breake on Thy Bier;
& y^s Beinge wolde fade att my laste fatall Sighe,
  & dyssolve withe my laste fallynge Tear.

Nowe Thy Cheekes are twyn Roses, & nowe Thine Eyes glowe
  Lyke ye Starres thro' ye Twylighte above;
Thou hast guess'd ye swete Name of y^s Beinge, I knowe,
  For Thy Blushes are breathynge, — 'T is Love.

ON THE DEATH OF A CLASSMATE.

Thou hast all seasons for thine own, O Death!

   Youth and the opening rose
May look like things too glorious for decay,
   And smile at thee, — but thou art not of those
That wait the ripened bloom to seize their prey.
                     MRS. HEMANS.

UNDERNEATH the crackling snow, while winter winds are sighing,
And the clouded light of day in the west is dying,
We have left her whom we mourn in solemn slumber lying.

As the morning glory blooms through the earliest hours,
As it withers ere the noon scorches leaves and flowers, —
So she bloomed and faded from this weary world of ours.

Faded — while through anxious months fears remained unspoken;
Faded — till the angel Death showed his ghastly token;
Then she breathed a sigh, and died, and our band was broken.

Nevermore we'll see her soul flash from that curtained eye!
Nevermore her marble cheeks resume their damask dye!
Nevermore her pallid lips part with a single sigh!

Glorious gleam the gates of pearl through which her soul has pressed;
Angels guard the jasper walls beyond whose borders blest
The wicked cease from troubling, and the weary are at rest.

But the love that cheered a life with her soul has fled;
Sorrow, by a stricken hearth, bows a mother's head;
For, O Death, thine arrow stings the living, not the dead.

REACTION.

SPRING breathes — her respiration breaks
  The melting coat of crusted snow;
She whispers — each blue violet wakes,
  The robins build, the roses blow:
Winter is past indeed! Life takes
  A fresher look, a brighter glow;
And in each heart the violet wakes,
  The robins build, the roses blow.

SOMNIA VANA.

Whether life may laugh or weep,
Death the true waking — life the sleep.
SIR E. B. LYTTON.

IN frail mortality's swift bark we glide
From its dark source down life's deceitful stream,
And while the keel cuts through the curling tide
We sleep, and idly dream.

Though in the quick round of youth's golden hours
The ruby lips of pleasure sweetest seem —
Crumbling to ashes 'neath the kiss of ours,
They leave a shattered dream.

First love entraps us in its magic snare: —
   Earth seems more blest and heaven appears more bright;
Suns pour a softer radiance through the air,
      And moons a milder light;

Our eyes find beauty in one only face,
   Our ears drink music from one only voice;
Love makes a paradise in every place
      That its first rays rejoice.

But death destroys, or time's rude hands unbind
   Each mystic bond that stays the starry beam;
Love's vision vanishes, and leaves behind
      The mockery of a dream.

Ambition lures our lagging steps to climb
   The craggy steep where fame's far honors gleam;
We gain the height, and find our sultry prime
      But gilds an idle dream.

So with each surge, that lifts the flashing keel,
   New visions rise till the last wave has fled,
And, ground to dust beneath death's iron heel,
      Our latest dream lies dead;

And evening's star shines through the sunset's gold
    And floods with flakes of pearl the silvery air;
And each fond dreamer's furrowed brow is cold
    Beneath his frosted hair.

Then through our eyelids glows a glorious ray
    Where life's last wave sobs on the sparkling shore,
And, in the splendors of eternal day,
    We wake, and dream no more.

REASSURANCE.

THREE thousand years ago king Solomon
Said, "There is nothing new beneath the sun."
Where, then, can I, amid the trite to-day,
Find a fresh thought to beautify my lay?

So cried a poet in acute despair;
And lo! an angel in the middle air,
Who heard with pity that despondent cry,
Suggested this encouraging reply:

Three thousand years ago king Solomon
Said, "There is nothing new beneath the sun."
Yet, as the lusty centuries unrolled,
Ilium's blind singer smote his harp of gold;

And Rome's sweet minstrel woke the silver strain
Whose accents linger yet in Art's domain;
And Avon's bard struck from his sunlit lyre
The diamond thoughts that gemmed each vibrant wire.

Down the long vista of departed years
Steals many a strain of trembling hopes and fears —
Each one imparting to the stormy breast
Its patient sorrow or its peaceful rest.

If they who sung had stayed for fresher thought,
They would have died, and left their tasks unwrought;
But who would leave a pathway that is fair
Because he sees another's footprint there?

Mark the example Nature sets each year,
When genial sunshine tells that Spring is near:
The vernal grass doth not refuse to grow
Because 't was grass that grew a year ago;

The leaves, the birds, the flowers, and the bees,
The morning sunbeams and the twilight breeze
Cease not to blow, to shine, to bloom, to soar,
Because the same has oft been done before.

Then care not if what thou dost yearn to say
Already has been said, but sing thy lay:
The thought, young poet, may be old, but he,
Who says it best, at last must owner be.

COULEUR DE ROSE.

EMBLEMS found not in the azure heaven,
  In the golden sun, the silver star,
On the bank with purple violets paven,
  In the milk-white petaled nenuphar;

Emblems found not in the emerald rushes,
  Mirrored in the wave that round them flows,
Live immortal in the vernal blushes
  Of the garden's queen — the crimson rose.

For those blushes symbolize the sources
  Of the life in earth, and sea, and air —
Breathing in unsyllabled discourses
  Of a beauty that is everywhere.

In each artery's pulsing current flashes
  Rosy tints that life imprisons there —
Tints it wooes within its myriad meshes
  From the crystal of the hueless air.

In the dark blue dome that o'er us closes,
  Gemmed with rolling worlds that gleam afar,
Sparkle through a veil of dewy roses
  Dawn's pale orb and evening's placid star.

All around us roseate dyes are glowing,
  In the earth below, the skies above;
But the tenderest tints in their bestowing
  Mantle softly o'er the cheek of love: —

Love that seeks the maiden in all ages,
  As the sunbeam seeks the rose's bud,
Till its rubric on her cheeks' pure pages
  Quivers warmly through in telltale blood: —

Love that bids through life its damask linger
  On that cheek from whose chill, changeless air
Death, with pallid brow and pulseless finger,
  Plucks the rose, and plants the lily there.

IN ACKNOWLEDGMENT.

[E. L. V.]

DEAD broke! not even a pothook left
  On which to hang a single letter!
Deprived of breath, of words bereft!
  A stammering, speechless, lucky debtor!

One moment since my teeming brain
  Held thought's wise owl and song's canary,
While, lately caged, a twittering train
  Of fancies filled its aviary.

But presto! mid the chirping birds
  In rushed your kindly wishes fluttering,
And soaring thoughts and winged words
  Have flown, and left me wildly stuttering.

O Venus, at thy throne I'll bend,
  And ever hymn thy beauty's praises,
If of thy stores thou wilt but lend
  Some honeyed words, some sugared phrases:

Or send the sunbeam of thy smile
  To thaw the ice of an "I thank you,"
And from the Tiber to the Nile
  O'er every goddess I will rank you.

Ah, Venus cannot hear my prayer;
  But if I look throughout creation,
Perhaps in earth, or sea, or air,
  I'll find a source of inspiration.

In vain! I gaze until the eye
  Is dazzled with the light, the motion,
Of sunlit leagues of azure sky,
  And billowy miles of dark blue ocean.

Can earth bestow what sky and sea
  Possess not in their ample dower?
Behold, as if to answer me,
  Upon the table blooms — a flower.

3

When language fails, when voices break,
  When eager lips are dumb with feeling,
Then Nature's radiant powers awake —
  Her silent eloquence revealing.

What faltering tongues cannot express
  Finds symbols in the garden bowers;
Take pity, then, on my distress,
  And read my thanks in these bright flowers.

TO IRENE.

IRENE, from what heaven afar
  Beams through the beauty of thy face
Thy spirit, like the silver star
  That brightens through the western space
Where sunset's radiant glories are?

Lo! framed in hyacinthine hair,
  I see thy lustrous loveliness;
It breathes of realms beyond the air,
  And makes our mortal mould express
Those looks that only angels wear.

BRYANTI MORS.

June 12, 1878.

. . . . .
'T were pleasant, that in flowery June,
. . . .
The sexton's hand, my grave to make,
The rich, green mountain-turf should break.

BRYANT.

VOLUPTUOUS month, whose golden hours
    With transient glory crown the year,
Thy daintiest buds and fairest flowers
    Must now adorn thy poet's bier;

Thy greenest turf must deck his grave;
 Thy gentlest rill must ripple there;
Thy grandest trees above it wave
 Their branches in the silvery air:

Thy bluest sky must o'er it bend
 In benediction from afar,
And day and night upon it send
 Thy softest rays from sun and star;
For all his purest, holiest love
 Around thy radiant beauties clung,
And sweet with strains inspired above
 For thee his saddest lay was sung.

He loved thee, for he loved all things
 Created by the hand of God —
The snow-crowned peaks, the icy springs,
 The fleecy clouds, the flowery sod,
The sky-bound prairie's billowy miles,
 The rushing streams, the restless sea, —
He looked, and lo! their sweeter smiles
 And brighter aspects came with thee.

He died as he had wished to die,
   While thy broad realms were all aflame;
Soft was the breeze and blue the sky
   When the destroying angel came;
Night lingered yet on land and sea,
   But heaven's bright morning shone for him—
That morning of eternity
   At which all earthly dawns grow dim.

SAINT AGNES.

WRITTEN AFTER SEEING G. G. FISH'S PICTURE.

I.

AROUND her head the furious flames are curling;
　Their fierce caresses seal her beauty's doom;
Yet through their smoky breath about her whirling
　She looks to heaven — forgetful of the tomb.

Beyond the gloom of death's unfolding portal
　She sees the radiance of unending day,
And glorious forms, unfading and immortal,
　That throng to greet her from life's weary way.

Unheeded, in the rapture of that vision,
　Are hate and torture, agony and death;
For starry Faith has shown the home elysian,
　Whose gates of pearl receive her parting breath.

II.

The tongues that mocked, the flames that marred her beauty,
  The malice, and the pain have passed away:
Yet still the solemn voice of sacred duty,
  That once she heard, we hear again to-day.

It never calls upon us now to vanquish
  The burning fagots and the blackened stake,
But to support privation, toil, and anguish
  Without a murmur, though the heart should break.

And ever when, oppressed beyond endurance,
  Our courage falters and our footsteps fail,
And even hope's bright rainbow of assurance
  No longer arches o'er life's darkened vale.

O star of Faith, o'er cloudy fears victorious,
  Burst through the rifts at last thy placid rays,
And lo! our wistful faces are made glorious:
  Death has no sting while on thy light we gaze.

PREMONITION.

WITH heart as free as wind or wave,
  I laugh at those whom Love beguiles,
And boldly mark and safely brave
    His most alluring smiles.

And yet I know she somewhere stands —
  She I shall love — my joy, my queen —
In what fair form, in what far lands,
    As yet unknown, unseen.

But I shall find her fairest face —
  Her glance will gleam upon my ken —
Somewhere — I know not in what place;
    Sometime — I know not when.

THE MIRROR.

[N. L. F.]

In my room, upon the mantel, rests a mirror in its frame;
And some gorgeous tiger-lilies, dashed with black and fringed with flame,
Mottled brown, and green, and golden, cluster gaily round the same.

Many quaint and curious objects are reflected in the glass;
Many faces peer into it; many sunbeams, and alas!
Many shadows there are mirrored as the hours slowly pass.

But the shadows and the sunbeams on its polished surface cast,
And the faces and the figures one by one go flitting past,
Till the silence and the darkness find it all unstained at last.

And the burning tiger-lilies, those in bud and those in bloom,
Never droop, nor wilt, nor wither in the hot air of my room —
In the sultry breath of summer — in the sunshine and the gloom.

Round the glass their glowing petals shine as fresh and bright of hue
As when they were first depicted by the skilful hand which drew
With a touch beneath whose magic leaves and flowers fairly grew.

May your life, O lovely artist, like the gift you gave to me,
While reflecting every object which around that life may be,
Always mirror heaven's true sunlight, while its shadows ever flee.

May your friendships, like the flowers that around the mirror twine,
Never fading, never changing, whether earthly or divine,
Round your whole existence cluster till its light has ceased to shine.

And as silently and slowly o'er that light the dark is cast,
May the manifold reflections one by one go flitting past,
And the white and dreamless angel find it all unstained at last.

A TOKEN.

I WATCHED beside her till the light
  Had slowly turned from gold to gray,
And beaming on the brow of night
  A star proclaimed the close of day;
But as the moon arose and threw
  In silvered outlines on the floor
The casement crossed with vines that grew
  About the blinds — I watched no more.

For life at last had left to death
  Her ransomed spirit's empty shell,
And unto me the fluttering breath
  And anguish of her last farewell:
I turned away, and yet the sting
  Was soothed, — for, as I turned, afar
The glitter of an angel's wing
  Shot downward from a distant star.

BIRTHDAY LINES

WRITTEN IN A COPY OF CLARKE'S "INDIAN SUMMER."

[L. I. F.]

DEAR Lillian, in this gift of mine
    Perchance a seer might see
On every leaf a happy sign
    Of what your life may be;
And, as he turned its pages o'er,
    Discern in sketch and rhyme
Bright symbols of that life before
    Its Indian Summer time.

Each printed page and painted leaf
  May represent a day
As bright and sweet, but not as brief
  And limited as they;
And when your book of life is bound —
  With months, and days, and hours
To fill its leaves — it may be found
  A book of songs and flowers.

But, as the present is the scope
  Of all that I can view,
My hearty wish and earnest hope
  Are always this — may you,
As long as flowers charm the sight,
  And songs enchant the ear,
Find them for aye as fresh and bright
  As in your eighteenth year.

TO Y^E GREY LADYE.

In sober Gowne of modeste Grey,
   & Hatt of Quaker hue,
I saw You passe, daie after daie,
   & did not dreame 't was You:
Forgive me, Love! How colde I tell
   Y^t You indeede were She
Whom I was soone to love soe well,
   & not ye Grey Ladye.

& yett before I knew 't was You,
  Ere yett I 'd even scann'd
Your darlynge Face soe fayre & treue,
  Or ever touch'd Your Hande,
I used to feele a sudden Thril
  Whenever You pass'd bye,
As iff my Hearte itselfe stood stil
  Because its Fate was nighe.

& when att laste We met, it seem'd
  As iff yᵉ Momente threw
Yᵉ Charme of alle I 'd thought or dream'd
  About love over You:
Yᵉ Sabbath glorie round You fell
  As iff it were Your Owne;
Yᵉ Musick of yᵉ Sabbath bell
  Seem'd rival'd by Your Tone.

I loved You — not as I have growne
  To love You synce — butt when
I first felte Your Hande in my Owne,
  Swete Hearte, I loved You then.

Y^e Love, wch first took Roote y^t Houre
   Soe many Months ago,
Through Winter storme & Summer shoure
   Hath never ceased to Growe;
Its glowynge Passion-floures before
   My Darlynge's Feet I caste,
For You to weare Forevermore,
   My First Love & my Laste.

4

O THOU ART LIKE A FLOWER.

FROM THE GERMAN OF HEINRICH HEINE.

O THOU art like a flower —
    As sweet, and pure, and bright;
I look at thee, and sadness
    Is mixed with my delight.

Methinks to lay my hand on
    Thy head would be but meet,
And pray that God may keep thee
    As bright, and pure, and sweet.

VALPINAR:

OR,

THE VISION.

All that I saw returns upon my view;
All that I heard comes back upon my ear.
WORDSWORTH.

VALPINAR:

OR,

THE VISION.

I.

I HAD a vision when the noonday sun
  Shot through my covert's leafy canopy
His scorching beams. A vapor, rolling dun,
  Had slowly wrapped in dim obscurity
Each varied scene that erst had charmed mine eye —
  The checkered sward, the glassy gliding stream,
The dale bedight with flowers, the turquoise sky,
  And in the distance, white and far, the gleam
Of snow-capped mountains.
                          But anon, the mist
  Rose like a curtain, and disclosed an old
  And ruined castle, gray with moss and mould,
And crumbled where the lips of countless years had kissed.

The shock of earthquake, or the wrath of man
 Had rent one tottering tower, and darkly yawned
 The ragged breach that ruthless might had spawned:
The crumbling battlements, the moat that ran
Below them, e'en the shaking turrets on a neighboring hill
Retained the scars of dire destruction still.

While wonder yet, or subtle charm compelled
 My tongue to silence, there approached me one
Whose bending body crowned by frosty eld
Announced a life nigh ended. In his hand
 A staff was feebly grasped, that, like a silent son,
Sustained him as he walked, and aided him to stand.
Youth, said the sage, thy spirit may be bold;
Yet from my spell thou canst not break until my tale is told.

II.

From sea to sea the name of Valpinar
  Was terrible: no chieftain dared dispute
  His potent blade. Throughout the mute,
Though populous land, from rising sun to evening-star,
  His dictate was the law; and men grew pale,
And trembled at his advent. Those afar
  Were governed by the iron flail
  Of disciplined despotism that makes the boldest quail.
And when, seizing the kingly purple, he
Hurled from the throne its crowned nonentity,
And thus o'ertopped the haughtiest in the nation,
None ventured to oppose his usurpation.

His skill, his valor, and his mighty name
  Awed neighboring nations into peace. O'er-seas
The orient galleys, deep with freightage, came;
  And commerce spread her canvas to the breeze;
The din of anvils followed that of arms,
  And useless cannon, turned to useful ploughs,

Furrowed the fallow land of countless farms,
And often ploughed the self-same spot
Where once had ploughed their smoking shot;
    And when the autumn sun on bending boughs
Looked down, and yellow fields, the useless swords
    Were hammered into sickles, and again
Throughout the land went hireling harvest hordes,
    And bearded grain was reaped instead of bearded men.

So peace and plenty crowned the smiling land:
    And Valpinar the king looked forth in pride,
    And marked the cheerful households far and wide,
And ruddy blazing hearths on every hand;
Then lifting up his eyes, he saw the wall
Encompassing the imperial capital,
And marked the marble palaces that rose
Amid the gardens, like the sparkling snows
On Himalaya's crest, or like the drifts
Of fleecy cloud that lie where morning lifts
Its gorgeous banners from the ocean bed;
And pride puffed up his heart, and the king said: —
" Is not this city great that I have built
    Of polished stone and marvelous masonry,

By might of mind, by blood like water spilt,
   And for the honor of my majesty!"
And while the words yet lingered on his lips,
His exultation suffered drear eclipse;
For from the heaven there fell a voice that said: —
   "Thine empire hath departed." And the king,
Trembling, confounded, gazed about in dread,
   But heard no further sound, and saw not anything.

Within the stately palace of his realm
   The king sat on his throne of gold in thought;
Fast-thronging fears combined to overwhelm
   His dauntless spirit, and his aspect caught
The quick contagion of his mood, for cold,
   And moist, and pale appeared his pensive brow
Beneath its royal weight of massy gold,
   Crusted with gems sufficient to endow
The daughter of a modern Crœsus, — bright
With many a ruby, pearl, and chrysolite.
Round him were ranged the pillars of his throne —
The men whose hearts and hands he trusted as his own;
His quick and crafty veteran counsellors,
All robed in rustling silks and glossy furs;

The captains of his legions cased in steel, —
Full-bearded, sunburnt, stout of heart, and leal.
A murmur in the distance stirred the air:
   Nearer it drew, and nearer, till the doors
Swung noiseless back, and up the marble stair,
   Through columned halls, o'er tessellated floors,
Advanced a knight in armor toward the king.
"To the usurper, Valpinar, I bring
Defiance from Omartes. There's my gage."
Loud on the pavement rang the warrior's wage,
And as it fell he slowly stepped aside;
But in his stead another stood, and cried: —
"I bear defiance from the king, Louchage,
To Valpinar the traitor. There's my gage."
And at his gauntlet's clang he strode away.
While these were speaking, o'er the ashen gray
Of Valpinar's pale cheek a flush had swept;
And as the last knight from the presence stept,
The king's hot anger fierce broke forth: — "What ho!
   Drag those audacious heralds back,
   And test their courage on the rack
   Till joints, and bones, and sinews crack:
We'll teach the miscreants manners — and yet, no!

A herald's rights are sacred. Let them go.
But on their kings shall fall the punishment and woe."
Then to the vast hall's vaulted roof arose
The shout of thousands: — "Woe unto our foes!"

Summer was wreathed in roses when the call
  Of war first roused the land to arms. The blows
Of flails announced the autumn festival,
  When Valpinar wooed battle from his foes.
Then shrilled the shout of onset; then on high
Glittered the golden gonfalons against the sky;
Then kettle-drums and brazen trumpets broke
The ominous silence, and far off awoke
The awkward culverins, and loudly pealed
Their sharp reports across the battle-field.
Then shook the ample plain beneath the shock
  Of rival armies met in full career;
Then did the opposing standards almost interlock
  O'er many a dinted shield and shivered spear;
Then rose the shriek of sudden death, the cry
For partial mercy, and the fierce reply,
The wounded charger's weirdly human neigh,
And all the mournful sounds that mark a fatal fray.

The battle's fate still in the balance hung,
When Valpinar upon his charger sprung, —
Marked where the banners of the allied kings
　　Swung in the sulphur of the battle-breeze —
Then as a swooping falcon swiftly wings
　　Upon its prey, or through the stormy seas
Cuts the stanch vessel's prow to port, he cleft
The mail-clad myriads as a weaver's weft,
And grasped the flag by which Omartes stood.
　　Above the quailing king his falchion swung
　　When in his ear the words of warning rung : —
" Thine empire hath departed."

　　　　　　　　　　　　　　Through his blood
An icy fear pulsated ; with a gasp,
He let both sword and banner drop from his nerveless grasp,
And, with a cry of anguish, turned and fled,
　　Leaving his captains palsied with dismay :
So, ere the twilight stars shone overhead,
　　His foes remained the victors of the day.

" Ay, 't is success makes right, and failure, wrong."
So Valpinar thought still, within his strong
Ancestral castle cooped by rebel bands

Of his own fickle subjects. At his hands,
While king, they had received all but their body's breath,
Yet now they clamored loud: — " Death to the tyrant, death ! "
  Long was the struggle; and the issue long
Was doubtful: but the wild besieging throng,
At length taught wisdom, concentrated all
Their heaviest ordnance on the curtain wall
Of yonder tottering tower; and when it fell,
Through yonder gaping breach, with fiendish yell,
The pack of human blood-hounds burst their way.
  Within the court-yard of the castle drew,
  Around their king, the last surviving few
Of those defenders who had kept at bay
The fiercest of the fierce assaulting band.
In swarmed the insurgent forces: hand to hand
The desperate struggle raged, and one by one
His faithful vassals fell, and Valpinar stood alone.
His king-like posture and his royal glance
  Compelled the awe-struck rabble to recede;
Above his head he poised a ponderous lance,
  That in his grasp did quiver like a reed;
But as he thus in act to fling it stood,
Once more he heard the words that chilled his blood: —

" Thine empire hath departed."

                       With a clang,
His bloodless weapon on the pavement rang;
His lightning glances wandering grew, and weak;
Dropped his raised arm, and paled his ruddy cheek;
Through his blue lips strange murmurs went and came,
And aguish tremblings shook his giant frame.
Then, with recovered courage, howled the rebel hordes: —
" Death to the tyrant!" And their thirsty swords
Drank deep the blood of Valpinar. But roar
And violence could trouble him no more;
The fearful strain at last had snapped the silver string,
And his proud spirit had already taken wing.
And when his helm was raised, around his brow
    The erewhile raven locks were blanched, for fear
    Had in an instant done the work of many a year,
And his once arrowy form was bent as now.

Behold, O youth, the ghost of Valpinar,
    Permitted in dim visions to recall
His warnful fate to those, whoe'er they are,
    That rest upon the spot which saw his fall
Thrice ninety years ago.

III.

              Slow from my sight
The vision faded, and the mist rolled down:
I woke, and in the west the sunset light
    Circled the hill-tops with a golden crown;
Across the dale, and o'er the glassy stream
Reflected sunbeams cast a yellow gleam;
And one lone mountain summit, white and far,
Glittered against the blue sky, like a star.